SQUINTY THE COMICAL PIG

RICHARD BARNUM

SQUINTY, THE COMICAL PIG

CHAPTER I

SQUINTY AND THE DOG

Squinty was a little pig. You could tell he was a pig just as soon as you looked at him, because he had the cutest little curly tail, as though it wanted to tie itself into a bow, but was not quite sure whether that was the right thing to do. And Squinty had a skin that was as pink, under his white, hairy bristles, as a baby's toes.

Also Squinty had the oddest nose! It was just like a rubber ball, flattened out, and when Squinty moved his nose up and down, or sideways, as he did when he smelled the nice sour milk the farmer was bringing for the pigs' dinner, why, when Squinty did that with his nose, it just made you want to laugh right out loud.

But the funniest part of Squinty was his eyes, or, rather, one eye. And that eye squinted just as well as any eye ever squinted. Somehow or other, I don't just know why exactly, or I would tell you, the lid of one of Squinty's eyes was heavier than the other. That eye opened only half way, and when Squinty looked up at you from the pen, where he lived with his mother and father and little brothers and sisters, why there was such a comical look on Squinty's face that you wanted to laugh right out loud again.

In fact, lots of boys and girls, when they came to look at Squinty in his pen, could not help laughing when he peered up at them, with one eye widely open, and the other half shut.

"Oh, what a comical pig!" the boys and girls would cry. "What is his name?"

"Oh, I guess we'll call him Squinty," the farmer said; and so Squinty was named.

Perhaps if his mother had had her way about it she would have given Squinty another name, as she did his brothers and sisters. In fact she did name all of them except Squinty.

One of the little pigs was named Wuff-Wuff, another Curly Tail, another Squealer, another Wee-Wee, and another Puff-Ball. There were seven pigs in all, and Squinty was the last one, so you see he came from quite a large family. When his mother had named six of her little pigs she came to Squinty.

"Let me see," grunted Mrs. Pig in her own way, for you know animals have a language of their own which no one else can understand. "Let me see," said Mrs. Pig, "what shall I call you?"

She was thinking of naming him Floppy, because the lid of one of his eyes sort of flopped down. But just then a lot of boys and girls came running out to the pig pen.

The boys and girls had come on a visit to the farmer who owned the pigs, and when they looked in, and saw big Mr. and Mrs. Pig, and the little ones, one boy called out:

"Oh, what a queer little pig, with one eye partly open! And how funny he looks at you! What is his name?"

"Well, I guess we'll call him Squinty," the farmer had said. And so, just as I have told you, Squinty got his name.

"Humph! Squinty!" exclaimed Mrs. Pig, as she heard what the farmer said. "I don't know as I like that."

"Oh, it will do very well," answered Mr. Pig. "It will save you thinking up a name for him. And, after all, you know, he does squint. Not that it amounts to anything, in fact it is rather stylish, I think. Let him be called Squinty."

"All right," answered Mrs. Pig. So Squinty it was.

"Hello, Squinty!" called the boys and girls, giving the little pig his new name. "Hello, Squinty!"

"Wuff! Wuff!" grunted Squinty.

That meant, in his language, "Hello!" you see. For though Squinty, and his mother and father, and brothers and sisters, could understand man talk, and boy and girl talk, they could not speak that language themselves, but had to talk in their own way.

Nearly all animals understand our talk, even though they can not speak to us. Just look at a dog, for instance. When you call to him: "Come here!" doesn't he come? Of course he does. And when you say: "Lie down, sir!" doesn't he lie down? that is if he is a good dog, and minds? He understands, anyhow.

And see how horses understand how to go when the driver says "Gid-dap!" and how they stop when he says "Whoa!" So you need not think it strange that a little pig could understand our kind of talk, though he could not speak it himself.

Well, Squinty, the comical pig, lived with his mother and father and brothers and sisters in the farmer's pen for some time. As the days went on Squinty grew fatter and fatter, until his pink skin, under his white bristles, was swelled out like a balloon.

"Hum!" exclaimed the farmer one day, as he leaned over the top of the pen, to look down on the pigs, after he had poured their dinner into the trough. "Hum! That little pig, with the squinty eye, is getting pretty big. I thought he was going to be a little runt, but he seems to be growing as fast as the others."

Squinty was glad when he heard that, for he wanted to grow up to be a fine, large pig.

The farmer took a corn cob, from which all the yellow kernels of corn had been shelled, and with it he scratched the back of Squinty. Pigs like to have their backs scratched, just as cats like to have you rub their smooth fur, or tickle them under the ears.

"Ugh! Ugh!" grunted Squinty, looking up at the farmer with his comical eyes, one half shut and the other wide open. "Ugh! Ugh!" And with his odd eyes, and one ear cocked forward, and the other flopping over backward, Squinty looked so funny that the farmer had to laugh out loud.

"What's the matter, Rufus?" asked the farmer's wife, who was gathering the eggs.

"Oh, it's this pig," laughed the farmer. "He has such a queer look on his face!"

"Let me see!" exclaimed the farmer's wife.

She, too, looked down into the pen.

"Oh, isn't he comical!" she cried.

Then, being a very kind lady, and liking all the farm animals, the farmer's wife went out in the potato patch and pulled up some pig weed.

This is a green weed that grows in the garden, but it does no good there. Instead it does harm, and farmers like to pull it up to get rid of it. But, if pig weed is no good for the garden, it is good for pigs, and they like to chew the green leaves.

"Here, Squinty!" called the farmer's wife, tossing some of the juicy, green weed to the little pig. "Eat this!"

"Ugh! Ugh!" grunted Squinty, and he began to chew the green leaves. I suppose that was his way of saying: "Thank you!"

As soon as Squinty's brothers and sisters saw the green pig weed the farmer's wife had tossed into the pen, up they rushed to the trough, grunting and squealing, to get some too.

They pushed and scrambled, and even stepped into the trough, so eager were they to get something to eat; even though they had been fed only a little while before.

That is one strange thing about pigs. They seem to be always hungry. And Squinty's brothers and sisters were no different from other pigs.

But wait just a moment. They were a bit different, for they were much cleaner than many pigs I have seen. The farmer who owned them knew that pigs do not like to live in mud and dirt any more than do cows and horses, so this farmer had for his pigs a nice pen, with a dry board floor, and plenty of corn husks for their bed. They had clean water to drink, and a shady place in which to lie down and sleep.

Of course there was a mud bath in the pig pen, for, no matter how clean pigs are, once in a while they like to roll in the mud. And I'll tell you the reason for that.

You see flies and mosquitoes and other pests like to bite pigs. The pigs know this, and they also know that if they roll in the mud, and get covered with it, the mud will make a coating over them to keep the biting flies away.

So that is why pigs like to roll in the mud once in awhile, just as you sometimes see a circus elephant scatter dust over his back, to drive away the flies. And even such a thick-skinned animal as a rhinoceros likes to plaster himself with mud to keep away the insects.

But after Squinty and his brothers and sisters had rolled in the mud, they were always glad when the farmer came with the garden hose and washed them clean again, so their pink skins showed beneath their white, hairy bristles.

Squinty and the other pigs grew until they were a nice size. They had nothing to do but eat and sleep, and of course that will make anyone grow.

Now Squinty, though he was not the largest of the family of pig children, was by far the smartest. He learned more quickly than did his brothers and sisters, how to run to the trough to eat, when his mother called him, and he learned how to stand up against one side of the pen and rub himself back and forth to scratch his side when a mosquito had bitten him in a place he could not reach with his foot.

In fact Squinty was a little too smart. He wanted to do many things his brothers and sisters never thought of. One day when Squinty and the others had eaten their dinner, Squinty told his brother Wuff-Wuff that he thought it would be a nice thing to have some fun.

Wuff-Wuff said he thought so, too, but he didn't just know what to do. In fact there was not much one could do in a pig pen.

"If we could only get out of here!" grunted Squinty, as he looked out through a crack in the boards and saw the green garden, where pig weed was growing thickly.

"Yes, but we can't," said Wuff-Wuff.

Squinty was not so sure about this. In fact he was a very inquisitive little pig--that is, he always wanted to find out about things, and why this and that was so, and what made the wheels go around, and all like that.

"I think I can get out through that place," said Squinty to himself, a little later. He had found another crack between two boards of the pen--a large crack, and one edge of the board was loose. Squinty began to push with his rubbery nose.

A pig's nose is pretty strong, you know, for it is made for digging, or rooting in the earth, to turn up acorns, and other good things to eat.

Squinty pushed and pushed on the board until he had made it very loose. The crack was getting wider.

"Oh, I can surely get out!" he thought. He looked around; his mother and father and all the little pigs were asleep in the shady part of the pen.

"I'm going!" said Squinty to himself.

He gave one extra hard push, and there he was through the big crack, and outside the pen. It was the first time he had ever been out in his life. At first he was a little frightened, but when he looked over into the potato patch, and saw pig weed growing there he was happy.

"Oh, what a good meal I shall have!" grunted Squinty.

He ran toward a large bunch of the juicy, green pig weed, but before he reached it he heard a dreadful noise.

"Bow wow! Bow wow! Bow wow!" went some animal, and then came some growls, and the next moment Squinty saw, rushing toward him Don, the big black and white dog of the farmer. "Bow wow! Bow wow! Bow wow!" barked Don, and that meant, in his language: "Get back in your pen, Squinty! What do you mean by coming out? Get back! Bow wow!"

"Oh dear! Oh dear!" squealed Squinty. "I shall be bitten sure! That dog will bite me! Oh dear! Why didn't I stay in the pen?"

Squinty turned on his little short legs, as quickly as he could, and started back for the pen. But it was not easy to run in a potato field, and Squinty, not having lived in the woods and fields as do some pigs, was not a very good runner.

"Bow wow! Bow wow!" barked Don, running after Squinty.

I do not believe Don really meant to hurt the comical little pig. In fact I know he did not, for Don was very kind-hearted. But Don knew that the pigs were supposed to stay in their pen, and not come out to root up the garden. So Don barked:

"Bow wow! Bow wow! Get back where you belong, Squinty."

Squinty ran as fast as he could, but Don ran faster. Squinty caught his foot in a melon vine, and down he went. Before he could get up Don was close to him, and, the next moment Squinty felt his ear being taken between Don's strong, white teeth.

"Oh dear! Oh dear! Oh dear!" squealed Squinty, in his own queer, pig language. "What is going to happen to me?"

CHAPTER II

SQUINTY RUNS AWAY

Between the barking of Don, the dog, and the squealing of Squinty, the comical pig, who was being led along by his ear, there was so much noise in the farmer's potato patch, for a few moments, that, if you had been there, I think you would have wondered what was happening.

"Bow wow! Bow wow! Bow wow!" barked Don, still keeping hold of Squinty's ear, though he did not pinch very hard. "Bow wow! Get back to your pen where you belong!"

"Squee! Squee! Squee!" yelled Squinty. "Oh, please let me go! I'll be good!"

And so it went on, the dog talking in his barking language, and Squinty squealing in his pig talk; but they could easily understand one another, even if no one else could.

Back in the pen Mrs. Pig suddenly awakened from a nap. So did Mr. Pig, and all the little pigs.

"Don't you hear something making a noise?" asked Mrs. Pig of her husband.

"Why, yes, I think I do," he answered slowly, as he looked in the feed trough, to see if the farmer had left any more sour milk there for the pig family to eat. But there was none.

"I hear someone squealing," said Wuff-Wuff, the largest boy pig of them all.

"So do I," said Squeaker, a little girl pig.

Mrs. Pig sat up, and looked all over the pen. She was counting her children to see if they were all there. She did not see Squinty, and at once she became frightened.

"Squinty is gone!" cried Mrs. Pig. "Oh, where can he be?"

The squealing noise became louder. So did the barking of the dog.

"Look, there is a board off the side of the pen," said Mr. Pig.

"Yes, Squinty wanted me to come outside with him," said Wuff-Wuff. "But I wouldn't go."

"Oh, maybe my little boy pig is outside there, making all that noise!" cried Mrs. Pig to her husband.

"Well, he isn't making all that noise by himself," said the father pig. "Someone is helping him make it, I'm sure."

They all listened, and heard the barking of Don, as well as the squealing of Squinty.

"Oh, some animal has caught him!" cried Mrs. Pig. Then she pushed as hard as she could with her nose, against the loose board near the hole in the pen, through which Squinty had run a little while before. Mrs. Pig soon knocked off the board, and then she ran out into the garden, Mr. Pig and all the little pigs ran after her.

The first thing Mrs. Pig saw was her little boy pig down on the ground in the middle of a row of melon vines, with Don holding Squinty's ear.

"Bow wow!" barked Don.

"Squee! Squee!" cried Squinty.

"Oh, you poor little pig!" grunted Mrs. Pig. "What has happened to you?"

"Oh, mamma!" squealed Squinty. "I--I ran out of the pen to see what it was like outside, and I was just eating some pig weed, when this big dog chased after me."

"Yes, I did," said Don, growling in his deep voice. "The place for pigs, little or big, is in their pen. The farmer does not want you to come out and spoil his garden. He tells me to watch you, and to drive you back if you come in it.

"This is the first time I have seen any of you pigs in the garden," went on Don, still keeping hold of Squinty's ear, "and I want you, please, to go back in your pen."

"Oh, I'll go! I'll go!" cried Squinty. "Only let loose of my ear, Mr. Dog, if you please!"

"What! Have you hold of Squinty's ear?" asked Wuff-Wuff. "Oh, do please let him go!"

"Yes, I will, now that you are here," said Don, and he took his strong, white teeth from the piggy boy's ear. "I did not bite him hard enough to hurt him," said Don. "But I had to catch hold of him somewhere, and taking him by the ear was better than taking him by the tail, I think."

"Oh, yes, indeed!" agreed Mr. Pig. "Once, when I was a little pig, a dog bit me on the tail, and I never got over it. In fact I have the marks yet," and he tried to look around at his tail, which had a kink in it. But Mr. Pig was too fat to see his own tail.

"So that's why I took hold of Squinty by the ear," went on Don. "Did I hurt you very much?" he asked the little pig who had run out of the pen.

"Oh, no; not much," Squinty said, as he rubbed his ear with his paw. Then, as he saw a bunch of pig weed close to him, he began nibbling that. And his brothers and sisters, seeing him do this, began to eat the pig weed also.

"Come! This will never do!" barked Don, the dog. "I am sorry, but all you pigs must go back in your own pen. The farmer would not like you to be out in his garden."

"Yes, I suppose we must," said Mrs. Pig, with a sigh. "Yet it is very nice out in the garden. But we must stay in our pen."

"Come, children," said Mr. Pig. "We must stay in our own place, for if we rooted up the farmer's garden, much as we would like to do it, he would have no vegetables to eat this winter. Then he might be angry at us, and would give us no more sour milk. So we will go back to our pen."

"Bow wow! Bow wow!" barked Don, running here and there. "I will show you the way back to your pen," he said, kindly.

And he capered about, here and there, driving the pigs back to the place where Squinty had run from, and where all the others had come from, to see what had happened to him.

The farmer, who was hoeing corn, heard the barking of his dog. He dropped the hoe and ran.

"Something must have happened!" he cried. "Maybe the big bull has gotten loose from his field, and is chasing someone with a red dress."

Into the garden he ran, and then he saw Don driving Squinty, and his brothers and sisters, and mother and father, back to the pen.

"Ha! So the pigs got loose!" the farmer cried. "Good dog! Chase 'em back!"

"Bow wow!" barked Don. "I will!"

But the pigs did not need much driving, for they were very good, and did not want to cause Don, or the farmer, any trouble if they could help it.

Soon Squinty and the others were safely in the pen again. The farmer looked at them carefully.

"So, you thought you'd like to get out and have a run, did you?" he asked, speaking to pigs just as if they could understand him. And they did, just as your dog understands, and minds you when you call to him to come to you.

"So you wanted a run in the garden, eh?" went on the farmer. "Well, I don't blame you, for it isn't much fun to stay cooped up in a pen all the while. But still I can't have you out. But I'll give you a nice lot of pig weed, just the same, for you must be hungry."

Then the farmer pulled up some more of the green stuff, and tossed it into the pen. He also gave them plenty of sour milk, which pigs like better than sweet milk. Besides, it is cheaper.

"Well, I guess you won't run away again," the farmer went on, as he nailed back on the pen the board which Squinty had pushed off. Perhaps the farmer thought one of the big pigs--the papa or mamma one--had made the hole for the others to get out. I am sure he never thought little Squinty, with his comical eye, did it. But we know Squinty did, don't we?

For some time after this Squinty was a very-good pig, indeed. Not that I mean to say he was bad when he ran out of the pen, for he did not know any better. But, after the board was nailed on tightly again, he did not try to push it off. Perhaps he knew he could not do it.

Squinty and his brothers and sisters had lots of fun in the pen, even if they could not go out. They played games in the straw, hiding away from one another, and squealing and grunting when they were found. They raced around the pen, playing a game much like our game of tag, and if they could have had someone to tie a hand-kerchief over their eyes, they might have played blind-man's buff. But of course they did not really do this.

However, they raced about, and jumped over each other's backs, and climbed upon the fat sides of their father and mother while the big pigs lay asleep in the shade.

Squinty was a pig very fond of playing tricks. Sometimes he would take a choice, tender piece of pig weed, which the farmer had tossed into the pen, and hide it in the soft dirt in one corner.

"Now see who can find it!" Squinty would call to his brothers and sisters, and they would hunt all over for it, rooting up the earth with their strong, rubbery noses.

Digging in the dirt was good practice for them, and their mother and father would watch them, saying:

"Ah, when they grow up they will be very good rooting pigs indeed. Yes, very good!"

Then Squinty, or his brothers or sisters, would root up the hidden pig weed, and the old pigs would go to sleep again, for they did not need to practice digging, having done so when they were young. About all they did was to eat and sleep, and tell the little pigs how to behave.

"Squinty, how is your ear that Don, the dog, bit?" asked Mrs. Pig of her little boy pig one day.

"Oh, it doesn't hurt me," answered Squinty. "Don did not bite very hard. He only wanted to catch me."

"Yes, Don is a good dog," said Mrs. Pig. "But you must be careful of other dogs, Squinty."

"Why, are not all dogs alike?" the little pig boy asked.

"Oh, no, indeed!" answered Mrs. Pig. "Some of them are very bad and savage. They would bite you very hard if they got the chance. So, whenever you see any dog, except Don, running toward you, run away as fast as you can."

"I will," promised Squinty. And he did not know how soon he would be glad to remember his mother's good advice.

For some days nothing much happened in the pig pen. Once or twice Squinty pushed his nose against the board the farmer had nailed on, but it was very tight, he found, and he could not push it off.

"Are you trying to get out again?" asked Wuff-Wuff.

"Oh, I don't know," Squinty would answer. "I think it would be fun if we all could; don't you?"

"No, indeed!" cried Wuff-Wuff. "Some big dog might chase us. I want to stay in the pen."

But Squinty was a brave, bold, mischievous little pig. He was not content to stay in the pen. He wanted to have some adventures. He wanted to get out in the garden, which looked so nice and green.

Squinty looked all around the other sides of the pen. He wanted to see if there was another loose board. If there was, he made up his little pig mind that he would go out again. But he said nothing of this to his brothers or sisters, or to his father or mother. He felt that they would not like him to go away again.

"But there is not much fun staying in the pen all the while," thought Squinty. "I wish I could get out."

Squinty, you see, had made up his mind to run away. Often horses run away, so I don't see why pigs can't, also. Anyhow, that was what Squinty intended to do.

But, for nearly a week after his first adventure in the garden, Squinty had no chance to slip out of the pen. All the boards seemed very tight.

Then, one day, it was very hot. The sun shone brightly.

"Dig holes for yourselves in the cool ground, and lie down in them," said Mrs. Pig. "That will cool you off."

Each little pig dug a hole for himself, just as a hen does when she wants to take a dust bath. Squinty dug his hole near the lower edge of the boards, on one side of the pen.

"I'll make a big hole," he thought to himself.

And, as Squinty dug down, he noticed that he could see under the bottom of the boards. He could look right out into the garden.

"That is very queer," thought the little pig boy. "I believe I can get out of the pen by crawling under a board, as well as by pushing one loose from the side. I'll try it." Squinty was learning things, you see.

So he dug the hole deeper and deeper, and soon it was large enough for him to slip under the bottom board.

"Now I can run away," he grunted softly to himself. He looked all around the pen. His father, mother, sisters and brothers were fast asleep in their cool holes of earth.

"I'm going!" said Squinty, and the next moment he had slipped under the side of the pen, through the hole he had dug, and once more he was out in the garden.

"Now for some adventures!" said Squinty, in a jolly whisper--a pig's whisper, you know.

CHAPTER III

SQUINTY IS LOST

This was the second time Squinty had run out of the pen and into the farmer's garden. The first time he had been caught and brought back by Don, the dog. This time Squinty did not intend to get caught, if he could help it.

So, after crawling out through the hole under the pen, the little pig came to a stop, and looked carefully on all sides of him. His one little squinty eye was opened as wide as it would open, and the other eye was opened still wider. Squinty wanted to see all there was to be seen.

He cocked one ear up in front of him, to listen to any sounds that might come from that direction, and the other ear he drooped over toward his back, to hear any noises that might come from behind him.

What Squinty was especially listening for was the barking of Don, the dog.

"For," thought Squinty, "I don't want Don to catch me again, and make me go back, before I have had any fun. It will be time enough to go back to the pen when it is dark. Yes, that will be time enough," for of course Squinty did not think of staying out after the sun had gone down. Or, at least, he did not imagine he would.

But you just wait and see what happens.

Squinty looked carefully about him. Even if one eye did droop a little, he could still see out of it very well, and he saw no signs of Don, the big dog. Nor could Squinty hear him.

Don must be far away, the little pig thought, far away, perhaps taking a swim in the brook, where the dog often went to cool off in hot weather.

"I think I'll go and have a swim myself," thought Squinty. He knew there was a brook somewhere on the farm, for he could hear the tinkle and fall of the water even in the pig pen. But where the brook was he did not know exactly.

"But it will be an adventure to hunt for it," Squinty thought. "I guess I can easily find it. Here I go!" and with that he started to walk between the rows of potatoes.

Squinty made up his little mind that he was going to be very careful. Now that he was safely out of the pen again he did not want to be caught the second time. He did not want Don, or the farmer, to see him, so he crawled along, keeping as much out of sight as he could.

"I wish my brothers, Wuff-Wuff or Squealer were with me," said Squinty softly to himself, in pig language. "But if I had awakened them, and asked them to run away with me, mamma or papa might have heard, and stopped us."

Squinty did not feel at all sorry about running away and leaving his father and mother, and brothers and sisters. You see he thought he would be back with them again in a few hours, for he did not intend to stay away from the pen longer than that. But many things can happen in a few hours, as you shall see.

"I won't eat any pig weed just yet," thought Squinty, as he went softly on between the rows of potato vines. "To pull up any of it, and eat it now, would make it wiggle. Then Don or the farmer might see it wiggling, and run over to find out what it was all about. Then I'd be caught. I'll wait a bit."

So, though he was very hungry, he would not eat a bit of the pig weed that grew near the pen. And he never so much as dreamed of taking any of the farmer's potatoes. He did not yet know the taste of them. But, let me tell you, pigs who have eaten potatoes, even the little ones the farmer cannot sell, are very fond of them. But, so far, Squinty had never eaten even a little potato.

On and on went the little pig, looking back now and then toward the pen to see if any of the other pigs were coming after him. But none were.

And there was no sign of Don, the barking dog, nor the farmer, either. There was nothing to stop Squinty from running away. Soon he was some distance from the pen, and then he thought it would be safe to nibble at a bit of pig weed. He took a large mouthful from a tall, green plant.

"Oh, how good that tastes!" thought Squinty. "It is much better and fresher than the kind the farmer throws into the pen to us."

Perhaps this was true, but I imagine the reason the pig weed tasted so much better was because Squinty was running away.

Perhaps you know how it is yourself. Did you ever go out the back way, when mamma was washing the dishes, and run over to your aunt's or your grandma's house, and get a piece of bread and jam? If you ever did, you probably thought that bread and jam was much nicer than the kind you could get at home, though really there isn't any better bread and jam than mother makes. But, somehow or other, the kind you get away from home tastes differently, doesn't it?

It was that way with Squinty, the comical pig. He ate and ate the pig weed, until he had eaten about as much as was good for him. And then, as he saw one little potato on the ground, where it had rolled out of the hill in which it grew with the others, Squinty ate that. He did not think the farmer would care.

"Oh, how good it is!" he thought. "I wish I had not eaten so much pig weed, then I could eat more of those funny, round things the farmer calls potatoes. Now I will have to wait until I am hungry again."

Squinty knew that would not be very long, for pigs get hungry many times a day. That is what makes them grow fat so fast--they eat so often. But eating often is not good for boys and girls.

Squinty had now come some distance away from the pen, where he lived with his mother, father, sisters and brothers. He wondered if they had awakened yet, or had seen the hole out of which he had crawled, and if they were puzzled as to where he had gone.

"But they can't find me!" said Squinty, with something that sounded like a laugh. I suppose pigs can laugh--in their own way, at any rate.

"No, they can't find me," thought Squinty, looking all around. All he saw were the rows of potato vines, and, farther off, a field of tall, green corn.

"Well, I have the whole day to myself!" thought Squinty. "I can do as I please, and not go back until night. Let me see, what shall I do first? I guess I will go to sleep in the shade."

So he stretched out in the shade of a big potato vine, and, curling up in a little pink ball, he closed his eyes, the squinty one as well as the good one. But first Squinty looked all around to make sure Don, the dog, was not in sight. He saw nothing of him.

When Squinty awakened he felt hungry, as he always did after a sleep.

"Now for some more of those nice potatoes!" he said to himself. He liked them, right after his first taste. He did not look around for the little ones that might have fallen out of the hills themselves. No, instead, Squinty began rooting them out of the earth with his strong, rubbery nose, made just for digging.

I am not saying Squinty did right in this. In fact he did wrong, but then he was a little pig, and he knew no better. In fact it was the first time he had really run away so far, and he was quite hungry. And potatoes were better than pig weed.

Squinty ate as many potatoes as he wanted, and then he said to himself, in a way pigs have:

"Well, I guess I'll go on to the brook, and cool off in the water. That will do me good. After that I'll look around and see what will happen next."

Squinty had a good nose for smelling, as most animals have, and, tilting it up in the air, Squinty sniffed and snuffed. He wanted to smell the water, so as to take the shortest path to the brook.

"Ha! It's right over there!" exclaimed Squinty to himself. "I can easily find the water to take a bath."

Across the potato field he went, taking care to keep well down between the rows of green vines, for he did not want to be seen by the dog, or the farmer.

Once, as Squinty was walking along, he saw what he thought was another potato on the ground in front of him. He put his nose out toward it, intending to eat it, but the thing gave a big jump, and hopped out of the way.

"Ha! That must be one of the hop toads I heard my mother tell about," thought Squinty. "I must not hurt them, for they are good to catch the flies that tickle me when I try to sleep. Hop on," he said to the toad. "I won't bother you."

The toad did not stop to say anything. She just hopped on, and hid under a big stone. Maybe she was afraid of Squinty, but he would not have hurt her.

Soon the little pig came to the brook of cool water, and after looking about, to see that there was no danger near, Squinty waded in, and took a long drink. Then he rolled over and over again in it, washing off all the mud and dirt, and coming out as clean and as pink as a little baby. Squinty was a real nice pig, even if he had run away.

"Let me see," he said to himself, after his bath. "What shall I do now? Which way shall I go?"

Well, he happened to be hungry after his swim. In fact Squinty was very often hungry, so he thought he would see if he could find anything more to eat.

"I have had potatoes and pig weed," he thought, "and now I would like some apples. I wonder if there are any apple trees around here?"

He looked and, across the field of corn, he thought he saw an apple tree. He made up his mind to go there.

And that is where Squinty made another mistake. He made one when he ran away from the pen, and another one when he started to go through the corn field.

Corn, you know, grows quite high, and pigs, even the largest of them, are not very tall. At least not until they stand on their hind legs. That was a trick Squinty had not yet learned. So he had to go along on four legs, and this made him low down.

Now he had been able to look over the tops of the potato vines, as they were not very high, but Squinty could not look over the top of the corn stalks. No sooner had he gotten into the field, and started to walk along the corn rows, than he could not see where he was going. He could not even see the apple tree in the middle of the field.

"Well, this is queer," thought Squinty. "I guess I had better go back. No, I will keep on. I may come to the apple tree soon."

He hurried on between the corn rows. But, though he went a long distance, he did not come to the apple tree.

"I guess I will go back to the brook, where I had my bath, and start over again from there," thought Squinty. "I will not try to get any apples to-day. I will eat only potatoes and pig weed. Yes, I will go back."

But that was not so easy to do as he had thought. Squinty went this way and that, through the rows of corn, but he could not find the brook. He could not find his way back, nor could he find the apple tree. On all sides of him was the tall corn. That was all poor Squinty could see.

Finally, all tired out, and dusty, the little pig stopped, and sighed:

"Oh dear! I guess I am lost!"

CHAPTER IV

SQUINTY GETS HOME

The rows of corn, in the field where Squinty the comical pig was lost, were like the streets of a city. They were very straight and even, just like the street where your house is, and, if you liked, you could pretend that each hill of corn was a house.

Perhaps Squinty pretended this, if pigs ever do pretend. At any rate the little lost pig wandered up and down in the rows of corn, peering this way and that, to see which way to go so he could get home again. He began to think that running away was not so much fun as he had at first thought.

"Oh dear!" Squinty grunted, in his funny, squealing voice. "I wonder if I'll ever see my mamma and papa again?"

Squinty ran this way and that up and down the rows of corn, and you can easily imagine what happened. He soon became very tired. "I think I will take a rest," thought Squinty, talking to himself, because there was no one else to whom he could speak. I think the little pig would have been very glad, just then, to speak even to Don, the dog. But Don was not there.

Squinty, wondering what happened to little pigs when they were lost, and if they ever got home again, stretched out on the dirt between two rows of corn. It was shady there, but over-head the hot sun was shining. Squinty's breath came very fast, just as when a dog runs far on a warm day.

But the earth was rather cool, and Squinty liked it. He would much rather have been down by the cool brook, but he knew he could not have a swim in it until he found it. And, just now, he seemed a good way off from it.

Poor Squinty! It was bad enough to be tired and warm, but to be lost was worse, and to be hungry was worse than all--especially to a little pig. And, more than this, there was nothing to eat.

Squinty had tried to nibble at some of the green corn stalks, but he did not like the taste of them. Perhaps he had not yet learned to like them, for I have seen older pigs eat corn stalks. And pigs are very fond of the yellow corn itself. They love to gnaw it off the cob, and chew it, just as you chew popcorn.

But the corn was not yet ripe, and Squinty was too little to have eaten it, if it had been ripe. Later on he would learn to do this. Just now he cared more about finding his way home, and also finding something that he could eat.

For some time the little lost pig rested on the cool earth, in the shade of the rows of corn. Then he got up with a grunt and a squeal, and began rooting in the ground.

"Perhaps I may find some potatoes, or some pig weed, here," thought Squinty. "Who knows?"

But all he could root up, with his queer, rubbery nose, was some round stones. Some of these were brown, and looked so much like the little potatoes, that Squinty tried to chew one. But when he felt the hard stone on his little white teeth he cried out in pain.

"Ouch!" squealed Squinty. "That hurt! Those are funny potatoes! I never knew they could be so hard."

Later on he learned that what he supposed were potatoes were only stones. You see it takes a little pig some time to learn all the things he needs to know.

Squinty let the stone roll out of his mouth, and he looked at it with such an odd look on his face, peering at it with his squinty eye, and with one ear cocked up sort of sideways, that, if you had seen him, you could not have helped laughing. No one could, if they had seen Squinty then, but there was no one in the field to watch him.

"Well," thought Squinty, after a bit, "this will never do. I can't stay here. I must try to find my way back home. Let me see; what had I better do? I guess the first thing is to find that field of real potatoes, and not the make-believe ones like this," and he pushed the stone away with his nose.

"When I find the potato field," he went on, still talking to himself, "I am sure I can find the brook where I had a swim. And when I find the brook I will know my way home, for there is a straight path from there to our pen."

So Squinty started off once more to walk through the rows of corn. As he walked along on his little short legs he grunted, and rooted in the earth with his nose. Sometimes he stumbled over a big stone, or a clod of dirt, and fell down.

"Oh dear!" exclaimed poor Squinty, when he got up after falling down about six times, "Oh dear! This is no fun. I wish I had stayed in the pen with my brothers and sisters. I wonder what they are doing now?"

Just then Squinty felt more hungry than ever, and he thought it must be feeding-time back in the pen.

"Oh, they must be having some nice sour milk just now!" thought Squinty. "How I wish I were back with them!"

And then, as he fancied he could smell the nice sour milk, which the farmer or his wife was pouring into the eating trough of the pen, Squinty just howled and squealed with hunger. Oh, what a noise he made!

Then this gave him an idea.

"Ha!" he exclaimed to himself, in a way pigs have, "why didn't I think of that before? I must squeal for help. My mamma, or papa, may hear me and come for me."

Then Squinty happened to think that the hole, by which he had gotten out of the pen, was not large enough for his fat papa or mamma to crawl through.

"No, they can't get out to come for me," Squinty thought. "They'll have to send Wuff-Wuff, or Squealer. And maybe they'll get lost, the same as I did. Oh dear, I guess I won't squeal any more. It's bad enough for me to be lost, without any of my brothers or sisters getting lost, too."

So Squinty stopped squealing, and walked on and on between the rows of corn, trying to find his way home to the pen all by himself. Squinty was really quite a brave pig, wasn't he?

By this time, as you can well believe, Mr. and Mrs. Pig, in the pen, had awakened from their afternoon sleep. And all the little pigs had awakened too, for they were beginning to feel hungry again.

"Isn't it about time the farmer came with some sour milk for us?" asked Mr. Pig of Mrs. Pig.

"I think it is," she said, looking up at the sun, for the sun is the only clock that pigs, and other animals, have. When they see the sun in the east, low down, they know it is morning. When it shines directly over their heads, high in the sky, they know it is noon. And when the sun sinks down in the west the pigs know it is getting toward night, and supper time.

The sun was low down in the west now, and Mr. and Mrs. Pig knew it must be nearly time for their evening meal.

"Come, Wuff-Wuff. Come, Squealer. Come, Squinty, and all the rest of you!" called Mrs. Pig in her grunting voice. "Come, get ready for supper. I think I hear the farmer coming with the nice sour milk!"

"Squee! Squee! Squee!" squealed all the little pigs, for they were very hungry indeed. "Squee! Squee! Squee!"

They all made a rush to see who would get to the eating trough first. Some of them even put their feet in, they were so anxious. Pigs are always that way. They know no better, so we must excuse them. If they had been taught not to do that, and then did it, we would not excuse them.

"Here comes the farmer with the sour milk," grunted Mr. Pig. "Oh, how good it smells!"

Just then Squealer cried:

"Why, where's Squinty?"

His brothers and sisters looked around.

Squinty, the comical pig, was not to be seen. But we know where he was, even if his mamma and papa and brothers and sisters did not. Squinty was in the cornfield, trying to find his way back to the pen.

"Why, where can Squinty be?" asked Mrs. Pig. "Squinty! Squinty!" she called, grunting and squealing as she always did. "Come to the trough!" she went on. "Supper is ready!"

But Squinty did not come. The farmer poured the sour milk down the slide, where it ran into the trough, and the little pigs began to eat. But Mr. and Mrs. Pig began looking for Squinty. They turned up the straw, thinking he might be asleep under it. No Squinty was to be seen. Then Mr. Pig saw the hole under the side boards of the pen.

"Ha!" exclaimed Mr. Pig, speaking to Mrs. Pig, "I think perhaps Squinty went out there."

"Oh, so he did!" said Mrs. Pig. "What shall we do?"

Just then the farmer looked over in the pen to see how fat the pigs were getting. He counted the little pigs. Then a queer look came over his face.

"Hello!" he exclaimed. "Only six here! One of those pigs has gotten out. I must look into this!"

Quickly he glanced all about the pen. He saw the hole out of which Squinty had run away.

"I thought so!" exclaimed the farmer. "One of the pigs has rooted his way out. I'll have to go after him. Here, Don!" he called to his dog. "A pig is loose! We must catch him!" and he whistled for the big black and white dog, who ran up, barking and leaping about.

At first Squinty's brothers and sisters were paying so much attention to drinking their sour milk, that they did not notice what the farmer said, even though they missed Squinty at the trough. But when they heard the dog barking, they wondered what had happened. Then they saw their mamma and papa looking anxious, and talking together in their grunting language, and Wuff-Wuff asked:

"Has anything happened?"

"Squinty is lost!" said Mrs. Pig, rubbing her nose up against that of Curly Tail, the littlest girl pig of them all. "He must have run out of the pen when we were asleep."

"Oh dear!" cried all the little pigs, and they felt very badly.

"Never mind," said Mr. Pig, "I heard the farmer call Don, the dog, to go off and find Squinty. I think he'll bring him back."

"Oh, but maybe Don will bite Squinty," said Wuff-Wuff.

"I guess not," answered Mr. Pig. "Don is a gentle dog. But, anyhow, we want Squinty back, and the only way we can get him is to have the farmer and his dog go after him."

The other little pigs finished their supper of sour milk, with some small potatoes which the farmer's wife threw in to them. Mr. and Mrs. Pig ate a little, and then the farmer, after stopping up the hole where Squinty got out, so no more of the pigs could run away, started off over the fields, calling to his dog.

"Bow wow! Bow wow! Bow wow!" barked Don. That meant, in dog language, "I'll find Squinty and bring him back."

Meanwhile Squinty had tried his best to find a way out of the cornfield. But all he did was to walk up one row, and down another. If he had been tall enough to stand up and look over the tops of the corn stalks, he might have seen which way to go, but he was not yet large enough for that.

Pretty soon Squinty looked up, and he saw that the sun was not as bright as it had been. Squinty knew what this meant. The sun was going down, and it would soon be night.

"Oh dear! I wonder if I shall have to stay out all alone in the dark night," thought poor Squinty. "Oh, I'll never run away again; never!"

Just then he heard, off through the rows of corn, a dog barking.

"Bow wow! Bow wow! Bow wow!" went the dog.

"Oh, what shall I do? Where shall I hide?" thought Squinty. "A bad dog is after me."

He ran this way and that, stumbling and falling down. The barking of the dog sounded nearer. Then Squinty heard a man's voice saying:

"Get after him, Don! Find him! Find that pig!"

"Bow wow!" was the barking answer.

"Ha!" thought Squinty. "Don! That's the name of the good dog on our farm! I wonder if he is coming after me?"

Just then the farmer, who had been following the tracks left in the soft ground by Squinty's feet, came to the cornfield. The farmer saw where the pig had been walking between the green rows of corn.

"He's here, somewhere, Don," the farmer said. "Find him!"

"Bow wow!" barked Don. "I will!"

Just then Squinty stumbled over a big stone, and he could not help grunting. He also gave a little squeal.

"Here he is, Don!" called the farmer. "Take him by the ear, and lead him back to the pen. Easy, now!"

Squinty stood still. He did not want to run away from Don. Squinty was only too anxious to be found, and taken home.

The next minute, through the rows of corn, came bounding Don, the dog. He was followed by the farmer.

"Ah, there he is! The little runaway!" cried the farmer man as he saw the pig. "After him, Don! But don't hurt him!"

Don raced up beside Squinty, and took him gently by the ear.

"Bow wow!" barked the dog, and that meant: "Come along with me, if you please. You have been away from your pen quite long enough."

Squinty gave a loud squeal when Don took him by the ear, but when the little pig found that the dog did not mean to hurt him, he grew quiet, and went along willingly enough.

"I must make that pig pen a great deal tighter, if they are going to get out and run away every day," said the farmer to himself, as he walked along behind Don and Squinty.

Soon they were at the pig pen, and Oh! how glad Squinty was to see it again. The farmer picked the little pink fellow, now all tired out and covered with dirt, up in his arms and dropped him down inside the pen with the other pigs.

"There!" cried the farmer. "I guess you'll stay in after this."

"Bow wow!" barked Don, jumping about, for he thought it was fun to chase runaway pigs.

And so Squinty got safely back home. But very soon he was to have some more adventures.

CHAPTER V

SQUINTY AND THE BOY

Did you ever have a little brother or sister who ran away from home, and was very glad to run back, or be brought back again, by a policeman, perhaps? Of course your little brother or sister may not have intended to run away, it may have been that they only wandered off, around the corner, toward the candy store, and could not find their way back again. But, when he or she did get home--how glad you were to see them! Weren't you?

It was just like that at the pen where Squinty, the comical pig, lived. When the farmer picked him up, and dropped him down among his brothers and sisters, in the clean straw, Wuff-Wuff, Squealer, and Curly Tail, and the others, were so glad to see Squinty that they grunted, and squealed and walked all over one another, to be the first to get close to him.

"Oh, Squinty, where were you?"

"Where did you go?"

"What did you do?"

"Weren't you awfully scared?"

"Where did the dog find you?"

"Did he bite you very hard?"

These were some of the questions Squinty's brothers and sisters asked of the little runaway pig. They pressed close up to him, rubbing their funny, wiggling, rubber-like noses against him, and snuggling up against him, for they liked Squinty very much indeed.

Then, after the young pigs had had their turn, Mr. Pig and Mrs. Pig began asking questions.

"What made you run away?" asked Squinty's papa.

"Oh, I wanted to have an adventure," said Squinty.

"Well, did you have one?" asked his mamma.

"Oh, yes, lots of them," answered the little pig. "But I didn't find very much to eat." Squinty was very hungry now.

"Oh dear!" exclaimed Mrs. Pig. "You are just too late for supper. It is all eaten up. We did not see that you were not here until too late. It's too bad!"

Squinty thought so himself, for the smell of the sour milk that had been in the feeding trough made him more hungry than ever.

Squinty walked over and tried to find a few drops in the bottom of the wooden trough. These he licked up with his red tongue. But there was not nearly enough.

"Ha! I guess that little pig must be hungry," said the farmer looking down in the pen, after he had put some more stones and a board over the hole where Squinty had gotten out. "I guess I'll have to feed him, for the others have had their supper."

And how glad Squinty was when the farmer went over to the barrel, where the pigs' feed was kept, and mixed a nice pailful of sour milk with some corn meal, and poured it into the trough.

"Squee! Squee!" cried Squinty as he made a rush over to get his supper.

"Squee! Squee!" cried all the other little pigs, as they, too, made a rush to get more to eat.

"Here! Hold on! Come back!" cried Mr. Pig. "That is Squinty's supper. You must not touch it. You have had yours!" and he and Mrs. Pig would not let Squinty's brothers and sisters shove him away from the trough. For sometimes pigs are so hungry that they do this, you know. Being pigs they know no better.

So Squinty had his supper, after all, though he did run away. Perhaps he should have been punished by being sent to bed without having had anything to eat, but you see the farmer wanted his pigs to be fat and healthy, so he fed them well. Squinty was very glad of that.

"Now all of you go to sleep," said Mrs. Pig, when it grew darker and darker in the pen. So she made them all cuddle down in the straw, pulling it over them with her nose and paws, like a blanket, to keep them warm. For only part of the pen had a roof over it, and though it was summer, still it was cool at night.

But Squinty's brothers and sisters had no notion of going to sleep so soon. They wanted to hear all about what had happened to him when he had run away, and they wanted him to tell them of his adventures. So they grunted and whispered among themselves.

"What happened to you, Squinty?" asked Wuff-Wuff.

"Oh, I had a fine swim in a brook," said Squinty.

"I wish that had happened to me," said Wuff-Wuff. "What else?"

"I found a nice field of corn," went on Squinty, "but I did not like the taste of it. I got lost in the cornfield."

"That's too bad," said Wuff-Wuff. "Did anything else happen?"

"Yes, I found some pig weed, and ate that, and some little potatoes."

"Oh, how nice!" exclaimed Twisty Tail. "I wish that had happened to me. Did you do anything else, Squinty?"

"Yes," said the comical little pig. "I saw something I thought was a potato, and it jumped away from me. It was a hoptoad."

"That was funny," said Squealer. "I wish I had seen it. Did anything else happen?"

"Yes," said Squinty. "I thought I saw another potato, but when I bit on it I found it was only a stone, and it hurt my teeth."

"That's too bad," said Wuff-Wuff. "I am glad that did not happen to me. Tell us what else you saw."

But just then Mrs. Pig grunted out:

"Come, now! All you little pigs must keep quiet and go to sleep. Go to sleep at once!"

So Squinty and the others cuddled closer together, snuggled down in the soft straw, and soon were fast asleep. Now and then they stirred, or grunted during the night, but they did not wake up until morning. They were running around the pen before breakfast, squealing as loudly as they could, for the farmer to come and feed them. But the farmer had his cows and horses and chickens to feed, as well as the pigs, and he did not get to the pen until last. And when he did, all the pigs were so hungry, even Mr. and Mrs. Pig, that they were squealing as hard as they could.

"Yes, yes!" cried the farmer, as though he were talking to the pigs. "I'm coming as fast as I can."

Soon the farmer poured some sour milk and corn meal down into the trough, and how eagerly Squinty and the others did eat it! Some of the smaller pigs even put two feet in the trough, they were so anxious to get their share. Squinty had an especially good appetite, from having run away, so perhaps he got a little more than the others.

But finally the breakfast was all gone, and the pigs had nothing more to do until dinner time--that is, all they had to do was to lie down and rest, or get up now and then to scratch a mosquito, or a fly bite.

"Well, I guess none of you will get out again," said the farmer, after a while, as he nailed a bigger board over the hole by which Squinty had gotten out. "Don, watch these pigs," the farmer went on. "If they get out, grab them by the ear, and bring them back."

"Bow wow!" barked Don, and that meant he would do as his master had told him.

For several days after this nothing happened in the pigs' pen except that they were washed off with the hose now and then, to clean them of mud and make them cool. Once in a while the farmer would take a corn cob and scratch the back of Mr. or Mrs. Pig, and they liked this very much. The other pigs were almost too little for the farmer to reach over the top of the pen.

One day the pigs heard merry shouts and laughter up at the farmhouse. There were the sounds of boys' and girls' voices. Then came the patter of many feet.

"Oh, look at the pigs!" someone cried, and Squinty, and his brothers and sisters, looking up, saw, over the edge of the pen, some boys and girls looking down on them.

"Oh, aren't they cute!" exclaimed a girl.

"Just lovely!" said another girl. "Pigs are so nice!"

"I wonder if any of them can do any tricks?" asked a boy who stood looking down into the pen.

"These aren't trained circus pigs," spoke one of the girls. "They can't do tricks."

The boy and the girls stayed for a little while, watching the pigs. Then the boy said:

"Let's pull some weeds and feed them."

"Oh, yes, let's!" cried the girls. The pigs were glad when they heard this, and they were more glad when the boy and the girls threw pig weed, and other green things from the garden, into the pen. The pigs ate them all up, and wanted more.

After that, for several days, Squinty and his brothers and sisters could hear the boy and the girls running about the garden, but they could not see them because the boards around the pig pen were too high. The boy and the girls seemed to be having a fine time.

Squinty could hear them talking about hunting the hens' eggs, and feeding the little calves and sheep, and riding on the backs of horses.

Then, one day Squinty looked up out of the pen, and, leaning over the top board he saw the farmer, the boy and another man.

"Oh, Father!" exclaimed the boy, "do let me have just one little pig. They are so nice!"

"A pig!" cried Father. "What would you do with a pig in our town? We are not in the country. Where would you keep a pig?"

"Oh, I could build a little pen for him in our yard. Look, let me have that one, he is so pink and pretty and clean."

"Ha! So you want that pig, do you?" asked the farmer. The boy and his father and sisters were paying a visit to the farm.

"Yes, I want a pig very much!" the boy said. "And I think I'd like that one," and he pointed straight at Squinty. Poor Squinty ran and tried to hide under the straw, for he knew the boy was talking about him.

"Oh, see him run!" cried the boy. "Yes, I think he is the nicest pig in the lot. I want him. Has he any name?"

"Well, we call him Squinty," the farmer said. "He has a funny, squinting eye."

"Then I'll call him Squinty, too," the boy went on. "Please, Father, may I have that little pig?"

"Well, I don't know," said his father slowly, scratching his head. "A pig is a queer pet. I suppose you might have him, though. You could keep him in the back yard. Yes, I guess you could have him, if Mr. Jones will sell him, and if the pig will behave. Do you think that little pig will be good, Mr. Jones?" asked the father of the farmer man.

"Well, yes, I guess so," answered the farmer. "He has run away out of the pen a couple of times, but if you board up a place good and tight, I guess he won't get out."

"Oh, I do hope he'll be good!" exclaimed the boy. "I do so want a little pet pig, and I'll be so kind to him!"

When Squinty heard that, he made up his mind, if the boy took him, that he would be as good as he knew how.

"When can I have my little pig?" asked the boy, of his father.

"Oh, as soon as Mr. Jones can put him in a box, so we can carry him," was the answer. "We can't very well take him in our arms; he would slip out and run away."

"I guess so, too," laughed the boy.

CHAPTER VI

SQUINTY ON A JOURNEY

"Mamma, did you hear what they were saying about Squinty?" asked Wuff-Wuff, as the boy and the two men walked away from the pig pen.

"Oh, yes, I heard," said Mrs. Pig. "I shall be sorry to lose Squinty, but then we pigs have to go out and take our places in this world. We cannot always stay at home in the pen."

"Yes, that is so," spoke Mr. Pig. "But Squinty is rather young and small to start out. However, it may all be for the best. Now, Squinty, you had better keep yourself nice and clean, so as to be ready to go on a journey."

"What's a journey?" asked the comical little pig, squinting his eye up at the papa pig.

"A journey is going away from home," answered Mr. Pig.

"And does it mean having adventures?" asked Squinty, flopping his ears backward and forward.

"Yes, you may have some adventures," replied his mother. "Oh dear, Squinty! I wish you didn't have to go and leave us. But still, it may be all for your good."

"We might hide him under the straw," suggested Wuff-Wuff. "Then that boy could not find him when he comes to put him in a box, and take him away."

"No, that would never do," said Mr. Pig. "The farmer is stronger and smarter than we are. He would find Squinty, no matter where we hid him. It is better to let him do as he pleases, and take Squinty away, though we shall all miss him."

"Oh dear!" cried Curly Tail, for she liked her little brother very much, and she loved to see him look at her with his funny, squinting eye. "Do you want to go, Squinty?"

"Well, I don't want to leave you all," answered the comical little pig, "but I shall be glad to go on a journey, and have adventures. I hope I don't get lost again, though."

"I guess the boy won't let you get lost," spoke Mr. Pig. "He looks as though he would be kind and good to you."

The pig family did not know when Squinty would be taken away from them, and all they could do was to wait. While they were doing this they ate and slept as they always did. Squinty, several times, looked at the hole under the pen, by which he had once gotten out. He felt sure he could again push his way through, and run away. But he did not do it.

"No, I will wait and let the boy take me away," thought Squinty.

Several times after this the boy and his sisters came to look down into the pig pen. The pigs could tell, by the talk of the children, that they were brother and sisters. And they had come to the farm to spend their summer vacation, when there was no school.

"That's the pig I am going to take home with me," the boy would say to his sisters, pointing to Squinty.

"How can you tell which one is yours?" asked one of the little girls.

"I can tell by his funny squint," the boy would answer. "He always makes me want to laugh."

"Well, I am glad I am of some use in this world," thought Squinty, who could understand nearly all that the boy and his sisters said. "It is something just to be jolly."

"I wouldn't want a pig," said the other girl. "They grunt and squeal and are not clean. I'd rather have a rabbit."

"Pigs are so clean!" cried the boy. "Squinty is as clean as a rabbit!"

Only that day Squinty had rolled over and over in the mud, but he had had a bath from the hose, so he was clean now. And he made up his mind that if the boy took him he would never again get in the mud and become covered with dirt.

"I will keep myself clean and jolly," thought Squinty.

A few days after this Squinty heard the noise of hammering and sawing wood outside the pig pen.

"The farmer must be building another barn," said Mr. Pig, for he and his family could not see outside the pen. "Yes, he must be building another barn, for once before we heard the sounds of hammering and sawing, and then a new barn was built."

But that was not what it was this time.

Soon the sounds stopped, and the farmer and the boy came and looked down into the pig pen.

"Now you are sure you want that squinty one?" the farmer asked the boy. "Some of the others are bigger and better."

"No, I want the squinty one," the boy said. "He is so comical, he makes me laugh."

"All right," answered the farmer. "I'll get him for you, now that you have the crate all made to carry him home in on the cars."

Over into the pig pen jumped the farmer. He made a grab for Squinty and caught him.

"Squee! Squee! Squee!" squealed Squinty, for he had never been squeezed so tightly before.

"Oh, I'm not going to hurt you," said the farmer, kindly.

"Squinty, be quiet," ordered his papa, in the pig language. "Behave yourself. You are going on a journey, and will be all right."

Then Squinty stopped squealing, as the farmer climbed out of the pen with him.

"At last I am going on a journey, and I may have many adventures," thought the little pig. "Good-by!" he called to his papa and mamma and brothers and sisters, left behind in the pen. "Good-by!"

"Good-by!" they all grunted and squealed. "Be a good pig," said his mamma.

"Be a brave pig," said his papa.

"And--and come back and see us, sometime," sniffled little Curly Tail, for she loved Squinty very much indeed.

"I'll come back!" said the comical little pig. But he did not know how much was to happen before he saw his pen again.

"There you go--into the box with you!" cried the farmer, as he dropped Squinty into a wooden box the boy had made for his pet, with a hammer, saw and nails.

Squinty found himself dropped down on a bed of clean straw. In front of him, behind him, and on either side of him were wooden slats--the sides of the box. Squinty could look out, but the slats were as close together as those in a chicken coop, and the little pig could not get out.

He did not want to, however, for he had made up his mind that he was going to be a good pig, and go with the boy who had bought him for a pet from the farmer.

Over the top of the box was nailed a cover with a handle to it, and by this handle the pig in the little cage could be easily carried.

"There you are!" exclaimed the farmer. "Now he'll be all right until you get him home."

"And, when I do, I'll put him in a nice big pen, and feed him well," said the boy. Squinty smacked his lips at that, for he was hungry even now.

"Oh, have you caged him up? Isn't he cute!" exclaimed one of the boy's sisters. "I'll give him the core of my apple," and she thrust it in through the slats of the box. Squinty was very glad, indeed, to get the apple core, and he soon ate it up.

"Come on!" cried the boy's father. "Is the pig nailed up? We must go for the train!"

"I wonder what the train is," thought Squinty. He was soon to know. The boy lifted him up, cage and all, and put him into the wagon that was to go to the depot. Squinty knew what a wagon was and horses, for he had seen them many times.

Then away they started. Squinty gave a loud squeal, which was his last good-by to the other pigs in the pen, and then the wagon rattled away along the road.

Squinty had started on his journey.

CHAPTER VII

SQUINTY LEARNS A TRICK

Squinty, the comical pig, tried to look out through the slats of the box, in which he was being taken away, to see in which direction he was going. He also wanted to watch the different sights along the road. But the sides of the farm wagon were so high that the little pig could see nothing. He stretched his fat neck as far as it would go, but that did no good either. Squinty wished he were as big as his papa or his mamma.

"Then I could see what is going on," he thought.

But just wishing never made anyone larger or taller, not even a pig, and Squinty stayed the same size.

He could hear the farmer and the children talking. Now and then the boy who had bought Squinty, and who was taking him home, would look around at his pet in the slatted box.

"Is he all right?" one of the girls would ask.

"He seems to be," the boy would say. "I am glad I got him."

"Well, he acts real cute," said another girl, who was called Sallie, "but I never heard of having a pig for a pet before."

"You just wait until I teach him some tricks," said the boy, whose name was Bob. "Then you'll think he's fine!"

"Ha! So I am to learn tricks," thought Squinty in his box. "I wonder what tricks are, anyhow? Does it mean I am to have good things to eat? I hope so."

You see Squinty, like most little pigs, thought more of something to eat than of anything else. But we must not blame him for that, since he could not help it.

Pretty soon the wagon rattled over some stones, and then came to a stop.

"Here we are!" called the children's father. "Bring along your little pig, Bob. Here comes the train."

"Ha! It seems I am to go on a train," thought Squinty. "I wonder what a train is?"

Squinty had many things to learn, didn't he?

The little pig in the box felt himself being lifted out of the wagon. Then he could look about him. He saw a large building, in front of which were long, slender strips of shining steel. These were the railroad tracks, but Squinty did not know that. Then all at once, Squinty heard a loud noise, which went like this:

"Whee! Whee! Whee-whee!"

"Oh my! what a loud squeal that pig has!" exclaimed Squinty. "He can squeal much louder than I can, I think. Let me try."

So Squinty went:

"Squee! Squee! Squee!"

And then the big noise sounded again, louder than before:

"Whee! Whee! Toot! Toot!"

"Oh my!" said Squinty to himself, snuggling down in the straw of his box. "I never can squeal as loud as that. Never!"

He looked out and saw a big black thing rushing toward him, with smoke coming out of the top, and then the big black thing cried out again:

"Whee! Whee! Toot! Toot!"

"Oh, what a terrible, big black pig!" thought Squinty. And he was a bit frightened. But it was not a big black pig at all. It was only the engine drawing the train of cars up to the station to take the passengers away. And it was going to take Squinty, also.

Squinty thought the engine whistle was a pig's squeal, but it wasn't, of course.

Pretty soon the train stopped. The passengers made a rush to get in the cars. Bob, the boy, caught up the handle of Squinty's box, and, after some bumping and tilting sideways, the little pig found himself set down in a rather dark place, for the boy had put the box on the floor of the car by his seat, near his feet.

And there Squinty rode, seeing nothing, but hearing many strange noises, until, after many stops, he was lifted up again.

"Here we are!" the little pig heard the children's papa say. "Have you everything? Don't forget your pig, Bob."

"I won't," answered the boy, with a jolly laugh.

"Well, I wonder what will happen next?" thought Squinty, as he felt himself being carried along again. He could see nothing but a crowd of persons all about the boy who carried the box.

"I don't know whether I am going to like this or not--this coming to live in town," thought the little pig. "Still, I cannot help myself, I suppose. But I do wish I had something to eat."

I guess the boy must have known Squinty was hungry, for, when he next set down the box, this time in a carriage, the boy gave the little pig a whole apple to eat. And how good it did taste to Squinty!

"Are you going to make a pen for him?" asked one of the boy's sisters, as the carriage drove off.

"Yes, as soon as we get to the house," said the boy.

By this time Squinty was thirsty. There was no water in his cage, but, a little later, when he saw through the slats, that he was being carried toward a large, white house, he was given a tin of water to drink.

"I'll just leave him in that box until I can fix a larger one for him," the boy said, and then, for a while, Squinty was left all to himself. But he was still in the box, though the box was set in a shady place on the back porch.

All this while Mr. Pig and Mrs. Pig, as well as the brother and sister pigs, in the pen at home, were wondering what had happened to Squinty.

"Where do you think he is now, Mamma?" Wuff-Wuff would ask.

"Oh, I don't know," Mrs. Pig answered.

"And will he ever come back to us?" asked Twisty Tail.

"Perhaps, some day. I hope so," said Mrs. Pig, sort of sighing.

"Oh, yes, I think he will," said Mr. Pig. "When he gets quite large the boy will get tired of having him for a pet, and perhaps bring him back."

"Were you ever carried off that way, Papa?" asked Grunter, as he rubbed his back, where a mosquito had bitten him, against the side of the pen.

"Oh, yes, once," answered Mr. Pig. "I was taken away from my pen, when I was pretty large, and given to a little girl for a pet. But she did not keep me long. I guess she would rather have had her dolls, so I was soon brought back to my pen. And I was glad of it."

"Well, I hope they will soon bring Squinty back," Wuff-Wuff said. "It is lonesome without him."

But, after a while, the other pigs found so many things to do, and they were kept so busy, eating sour milk, and getting fat, that they nearly forgot about Squinty.

But, all this time, something was happening to the comical little pig.

Toward evening of the first day that Squinty had been put in the new little cage, the boy, who had not been near him in some time, came back to look at his pet.

"Now I have a larger place for you," the boy said, speaking just as though Squinty could understand him. And, in fact, Squinty did know much of what was said to him, though he could not talk back in boy language, being able to speak only his own pig talk.

"And I guess you are hungry, too, and want something to eat," the boy went on. "I will feed you!"

"Squee! Squee! Squee!" squealed Squinty. If there was one word in man-talk that he understood very well, it was "feed." He had often heard the farmer say:

"Well, now I must feed the pigs."

And right after that, some nice sour milk would come splashing down into the trough of the pen. So when Squinty heard the word "feed" again, he guessed what was going to happen.

And he guessed right, too.

The boy picked Squinty up, box and all, and carried him to the back yard.

"Now I'll give you more room to run about, and then I'll have a nice supper for you," the boy said, talking to his little pig just as you would to your dog, or kittie.

With a hammer the boy knocked off some of the slats of the small box in which Squinty had made his journey. Then the boy lifted out the comical little pig, and Squinty found himself inside a large box, very much like the pen at home. It had clean straw in it, and a little trough, just like the one at his "home," where he could eat. But there was nothing in the trough to eat, as yet, and the box seemed quite lonesome, for Squinty was all alone.

"Here you are now! Some nice sour milk, and boiled potatoes!" cried the boy, and then Squinty smelled the most delicious smell--to him at least. Down into the trough came the sour milk and potatoes.

"Squee! Squee!" yelled Squinty in delight, And how fast he ate! That was because he was hungry, you see, but pigs nearly always eat fast, as though they were continually in a hurry.

"Oh, isn't it cute!" exclaimed a voice over Squinty's head. He looked up, half shutting his one funny eye, and cocking one ear up, and letting the other droop down. But he did not stop eating.

"Oh, isn't he funny!" cried another voice. And Squinty saw the boy and his sisters looking at him.

"Yes, he surely is a nice pig," the boy said, "In a few days, when he gets over being strange, I'm going to teach him some tricks."

"Ha! There's that word tricks again!" thought Squinty. "I wonder what tricks are? But I shall very soon find out."

For a few days Squinty was rather lonesome in his new pen, all by himself. He missed his papa and mamma and brothers and sisters. But the boy came to see Squinty every day, bringing him nice things to eat, and, after a bit, Squinty came to look for his new friend.

"I guess you are getting to know me, aren't you, old fellow?" the boy said one day, after feeding Squinty, and he scratched the little pig on the back with a stick.

"Uff! Uff!" grunted Squinty. That, I suppose, was his way of saying:

"Of course I know you, and I like you, boy."

One day, about a week after he had come to his new home, Squinty heard the boy say:

"Now I think you are tame enough to be let out. I don't believe you will run away, will you? But, anyhow, I'll tie a string to your leg, and then you can't."

Squinty wished he could speak boy language, and tell his friend that he would not run away as long as he was kindly treated, but of course Squinty could not do this. Instead, he could only grunt and squeal.

The boy tied a string to Squinty's leg, and let him out of the pen. The comical little pig was glad to have more room in which to move about. He walked first to one side, and then the other, rooting in the dirt with his funny, rubbery nose. The boy laughed to see him.

"I guess you are looking for something to eat," the boy said. "Well, let's see if you can find these acorns."

The boy hid them under a pile of dirt, and watched. Squinty smelled about, and sniffed. He could easily tell where the acorns had been hidden, and, a moment later, he had rooted them up and was eating them.

"Oh, you funny little pig!" cried the boy. "You are real smart! You know how to find acorns. That is one trick."

"Ha! If that is a trick, it is a very easy one--just rooting up acorns," thought Squinty to himself.

Squinty walked around, as far as the rope tied to his leg would let him. The other end of the rope was held by the boy. Once the rope got tangled around Squinty's foot, and he jumped over it to get free. The boy saw him and cried:

"Oh, I wonder if I could teach you to jump the rope? That would be a fine trick. Let me see."

The boy thought a moment, and then lifted Squinty up, and set him down on one side of the rope, which he raised a little way from the ground, just as girls do when they are playing a skipping game.

On the other side of the rope the boy put an apple.

"Now, Squinty," said Bob, "if you want that apple you must jump the rope to get it. Come on."

At first Squinty did not understand what was wanted of him. He saw nothing but the apple, and thought how much he wanted it. He started for it, but, before he could get it the boy pulled up the rope in front of him. The rope stopped Squinty.

"Jump over the rope if you want the apple," said the boy. Of course Squinty could not exactly understand this talk. He tried once more to get the apple, but, every time he did, he found the rope in front of him, in the way.

"Well!" exclaimed Squinty to himself, "I am going to get that apple, rope or no rope. I guess I'll have to get over the rope somehow."

So the next time he started for the juicy apple, and the rope was pulled up in front of him, Squinty gave a little spring, and over the rope he went, jumping with all four legs, coming down on the other side, like a circus man jumping over the elephant's back.

"Oh, fine! Good!" cried the boy, clapping his hands. "Squinty has learned to do another trick!"

"Uff! Uff!" grunted Squinty, as he chewed the apple. "So that's another trick, is it?"

CHAPTER VIII

SQUINTY IN THE WOODS

Bob, the boy who had bought Squinty, the comical pig, laughed and clapped his hands. His two sisters, who were playing with their dolls in the shade of an evergreen tree, heard their brother, and one of them called out:

"What is it, Bob? What is it?"

"Oh, come and see my pig do a trick!" answered the boy. "He is too funny for anything!"

"Can he really do a trick?" asked the smaller sister, whose name was Mollie.

"Indeed he can," the boy said. "He can do two tricks--find hidden acorns, and jump a rope."

"Oh, no, not really jump a rope!" cried Sallie.

"You just come and see!" the boy called.

All this while Squinty was chewing on the apple which he had picked up from the ground after he had jumped over the rope. He heard what the boy said, and Squinty made up his mind.

"Well," said the little pig to himself, "if it is any fun for that boy and his sisters to watch me jump over a rope, and dig up acorns, I don't mind doing it for them. They call them tricks, but I call it getting something to eat."

And they were both right, you see.

Sallie and Mollie, the two sisters, laid down their dolls in the shade, and ran over toward their brother, who still held one end of the rope, that was fast to Squinty's leg.

"Make him do some tricks for us," begged Mollie.

"Show us how he jumps the rope," said Sallie.

"First, I'll have him dig up the acorns, as that's easier," spoke Bob. "Here, Squinty!" he called. "Find the acorns! Find 'em!"

While Squinty had been munching on the apple, the boy had dug a hole, put some sweet acorn nuts into it, and covered them up with dirt. Squinty had not seen him do this, but Squinty thought he could find the nuts just the same.

There were two ways of doing this. Squinty had a very sharp-smelling nose. He could smell things afar off, that neither you nor I could smell even close by. And Squinty could also tell, by digging in the ground with his queer, rubbery nose, just where the ground was soft and where it was hard. And he knew it would be soft at the place where the boy had dug a hole in which to hide the acorns.

So, when Bob called for Squinty to come and find the acorn nuts, even though the little pig had not seen just where they were hidden, Squinty felt sure he could dig them up.

"He'll never find them!" said Sallie.

"Just you watch!" exclaimed the boy.

He pulled on the rope around Squinty's leg. At first the little pig was not quite sure what was wanted of him. He thought perhaps he was to jump over the rope after another apple. But he saw no fruit waiting for him. Then he looked carefully about and smelled the air. The boy was very gentle with him, and waited patiently.

And I might say, right here, that if you ever try to teach your pets any tricks, you must be both kind and gentle with them, for you know they are not as smart as you are, and cannot think as quickly.

"Ha! I smell acorns!" thought Squinty to himself. "I guess the boy must want me to do the first trick, as he calls it, and dig up the acorns. I'll do it!"

Carefully Squinty sniffed the air. When he turned one way he could smell the acorns quite plainly. When he turned the other way he could not smell them quite so well. So he started off in the direction where he could most plainly smell the nuts he loved so well.

Next he began rooting in the ground. At first it was very hard for his nose, but soon it became soft. Then he could smell the acorns more plainly than before.

"See, he is going right toward them!" cried the boy.

"There, he has them!" exclaimed Sallie.

"Oh, so he has!" spoke Mollie. "I wouldn't have thought he could!"

And, by that time, Squinty had found the hole where the boy had covered the acorns with dirt, and Squinty was chewing the sweet nuts.

"Now make him jump the rope," said Mollie.

"I will, as soon as he eats the acorns," replied the boy.

"Ha! I am going to have another apple, just for jumping a rope," thought Squinty, in delight.

You see the little pig imagined the trick was done just to get him to eat the apple. He did not count the rope-jumping part of it at all, though that, really, was what the boy wanted.

Once more Bob placed the apple on the ground, on the far side of the rope. One end of the rope the boy held in his hand, and the other was around Squinty's leg, but a loop of it was made fast to a stick stuck in the ground, so the boy could pull on the rope and raise or lower it, just as you girls do when you play.

"Come on, now, Squinty! Jump over it!" called the boy.

The little pig saw the apple, and smelled it. He wanted very much to get it. But, when he ran toward it, he found the rope raised up in front of him. He forgot, for a moment, his second trick, and stood still.

"Oh, I thought you said he would jump the rope!" said Mollie, rather disappointed.

"He will--just wait a minute," spoke the boy. "Come on, Squinty!" he called.

Once more Squinty started for the apple. This time he remembered that, before, he had to jump the rope to get it. So he did it again. Over the rope he went, with a little jump, coming down on the side where the apple was, and, in a second he was chewing the juicy fruit.

"There!" cried the boy. "Didn't he jump the rope?"

"Oh, well, but he didn't jump it fast, back and forth, like we girls do," said Mollie.

"But it was pretty good--for a little pig," said Sallie.

"I think so, too," spoke the boy. "And I am going to teach him to jump real fast, and without going for an apple each time. I'm going to teach him other tricks, too."

"Oh dear!" thought Squinty, when he heard this. "So I am to learn more tricks, it seems. Well, I hope they will all be eating ones."

"Make him do it again," suggested Mollie, after a bit.

"No, I haven't any more apples," the boy answered. "And at first I'll have to make him jump for an apple each time. After a bit I'll not give him an apple until he has done all his tricks. Come on now, Squinty, back to your pen."

The boy lifted up his pet, and put him back in the pen that had been especially built for the little pig. As soon as he was in it Squinty ran over to the trough, hoping there would be some sour milk in it. But there was none.

"You've had enough to eat for a while," said the boy with a laugh. "Later on I'll give you your milk."

"Uff! Uff!" grunted Squinty, and I suppose he meant he would be glad to have the milk now. But he got none, so he curled himself up in the clean straw and went to sleep.

When he awakened, he thought at first he was back in the pen at home, and he cried out:

"Oh, Wuff-Wuff! Oh, Twisty Tail. I had the queerest dream! I thought a boy had me, and that I could jump a rope, and hunt acorns, and do lots of tricks. But I--!" And then Squinty stopped. He looked around and found himself all alone in the new pen. None of his brothers or sisters was near him, and he could not hear his mamma or papa grunting near the feed trough.

"Ha! It wasn't a dream, after all," thought Squinty, a bit sorrowfully. "It's all real--I can do tricks, and a boy has me."

Every few days after that the boy took Squinty out of his pen, and let him do the rope-jumping and the acorn-hunting tricks. And it did not take Squinty long to learn to jump the rope when there was no apple on the other side. The boy would say:

"Jump over the rope, Squinty!"

And over it the little pig would go. But if he did not get the apple as soon as he jumped, he did get it afterward, which was just as good. It was sort of a reward for his tricks, you see.

"Now you must learn a new trick," said the boy one day. "I want you to learn how to walk on your hind legs, Squinty. It is not going to be easy, either. But I guess you can do it. And I am going to take the rope off your leg, for I do not believe you will run away from me now."

So the rope was taken off Squinty's leg. And he liked the boy so much, and liked his new home, and the nuts and apples he got to eat were so good, that Squinty did not try to run away.

"Up on your hind legs!" cried the boy, and, by taking hold of Squinty's front feet, Bob raised his pet up on the hind legs.

"Now stand there!" the boy cried, but when he took away his hands of course Squinty came down on all four legs. He did not know what the boy meant to have him do.

"I guess I'll have to stand you in a corner to start with," the boy said. "That will brace you up."

Then, kindly and gently, the boy took Squinty over to the place where the corn crib was built on to the barn. This made a corner and the little pig was stood up on his hind legs in that. Then, with something to lean his back against, he did not feel like falling over, and he remained standing up on two legs, with his front feet stuck out in front of him.

"That's the way to do it!" cried Bob. "Soon you will be able to stand up without anything to lean against. And, a little later, you will be able to walk on your hind legs. Now here's an apple for you, Squinty!"

So you see Squinty received his reward for starting to learn a new trick.

In a few days, just as the boy had said, the little pig found that he could sit up on his hind legs all alone, without anything to lean back against.

But learning to walk on his hind legs was a little harder.

The boy, however, was patient and kind to him. At first Bob held Squinty's front feet, and walked along with him so the little pig would get used to the new trick. Then one day Bob said:

"Now, Squinty, I want you to walk to me all by yourself. Stand up!"

Squinty stood up on his hind legs. The boy backed away from him, and stood a little distance off, holding out a nice, juicy potato this time.

"Come and get the potato," called the boy.

"Squee! Squee!" grunted Squinty. "I can't!" I suppose he meant to say.

"Come on!" cried the boy. "Don't be afraid. You can do it!"

Squinty wanted that potato very much. And the only way to get it was to walk to it on his hind legs. If he let himself down on all four legs he knew the boy would not give him the potato. So Squinty made up his little pig mind that he would do this new trick.

Off he started, walking by himself on his hind legs, just like a trained bear.

"Fine! That's the way to do it! I knew you could!" the boy cried when Squinty reached him, and took the potato out of his hand. "Good little pig!" and he scratched Squinty's back with a stick.

"Uff! Uff!" squealed Squinty, very much pleased.

And from then on the comical little pig learned many tricks.

He could stand up a long time, on his hind legs, with an apple on his nose. And he would not eat it until the boy called:

"Now, Squinty!"

Then Squinty would toss the apple up in the air, off his nose, and catch it as it came down. Oh, how good it tasted!

Squinty also learned to march around with a stick for a gun, and play soldier. He liked this trick best of all, for he always had two apples to eat after that.

Many of Bob's boy friends came to see his trained pig. They all thought he was very funny and cute, and they laughed very hard when Squinty looked at them with his queer, drooping eye. They would feed him apples, potatoes and sometimes bits of cake that Bob's mother gave them. Squinty grew very fond of cake.

Then one day something happened. Bob always used to lock the door of the new pig pen every night, for, though he knew his pet was quite tame now, he thought, if the door were left open, Squinty might wander away. And that is exactly what Squinty did. He did not mean to do wrong, but he knew no better. One evening, after he had done many tricks that day, when Squinty found the door of his pen part way open, he just pushed it the rest of the way with his strong nose, and out he walked! No one saw him.

"Uff! Uff!" grunted Squinty, looking about, "I guess I'll go take a walk by myself. I may find something good to eat."

Out of the pen he went. There was no garden here, such as the farmer had at Squinty's first home. But, not far from the pig pen was the big, green wood.

"I'll go over in there and see what happens," thought Squinty. "Perhaps I may find some acorns."

And so Squinty ran away to the woods.

CHAPTER IX

SQUINTY'S BALLOON RIDE

This was the third time Squinty had run away. But not once did he intend to do any wrong; you see he knew no better. He just found his pen door open and walked out--that was all there was to it.

"I wonder what will happen to me this time?" thought the comical little pig, as he hurried along over the ground, toward the woods. "I don't believe Don, the dog, will find me here, for he must be back on the farm. But some other dog might. I had better be careful, I guess."

When Squinty thought this he stopped and looked carefully around for any signs of a barking dog. But he saw none. It was very still and quiet, for it was nearly supper time in the big house where Bob lived, and he and his sisters were waiting for the bell to ring to call them to the table.

But Squinty had had his supper, and, for the time, he was not hungry.

"And if I do get hungry again, I may find something in the woods," he said to himself. "Acorn nuts grow in the woods, and they are very good. I'll root up some of them."

Once or twice Squinty looked back toward the pen he had run away from, to see if Bob, his master, were coming after him. But Bob had no idea his little pet had run away. In fact, just then, Bob was wondering what new trick he could teach Squinty the next day.

On and on ran the comical pig. Once he found something round and yellow on the ground.

"Ha! That looks like a yellow apple," thought Squinty, and he bit it hard with his white teeth. Then his mouth all puckered up, he felt a sour taste, and he cried out:

"Wow! I don't like that. Oh, that isn't an apple at all!"

And it wasn't--it was a lemon the grocery boy had dropped.

"Oh! How sour!" grunted Squinty. "I'd like a drink of water to take the taste of that out of my mouth."

Squinty lifted his nose up in the air, and sniffed and snuffed. He wanted to try to smell a spring of water, and he did, just on the edge of the big wood. Over to the spring he ran on his little short legs, and soon he was having a fine drink.

"Now I feel better," Squinty said. "What will happen next?"

Nothing did for some time, and, when it did it was so strange that Squinty never forgot it as long as he lived. I'll tell you all about it.

He walked on through the woods, Squinty did, and, before very long, he found some acorns. He ate as many as he wanted and then, as he always felt sleepy after he had eaten, he thought he would lie down and have a nap.

He found a place, near a big stump, where there was a soft bed of dried leaves, nearly as nice as his straw bed in the pen at home. On this he stretched out, and soon he was fast asleep.

When Squinty awoke it was real dark. He jumped up with a little grunt, and said to himself:

"Well, I did not mean to stay away from my pen so long. I guess I had better go back."

Squinty started to go back the way he had come, but I guess you can imagine what happened. It was so dark he could not find the path. He walked about, stumbling over sticks and stones and stumps, sometimes falling down on soft moss, and again on the hard ground. Finally Squinty thought:

"Well, it is of no use. I can't get back tonight, that is sure. I shall have to stay here. Oh dear! I hope there are no dogs to bite me!"

Squinty listened carefully. He could hear no barks. He hunted around in the dark until he found another soft bed of leaves, and on that he cuddled himself up to go to sleep for the night. He was a little afraid, but, after all, he was used to sleeping alone, and, even though he was outside of his pen now, he did not worry much.

"In the morning I shall go back to the boy who taught me tricks," thought Squinty.

But something else happened in the morning.

Squinty was awake when the sun first peeped up from behind the clouds. The little pig scratched his ear, where a mosquito had bitten him during the night. Then he stretched first one leg and then the others, and said:

"Ha! Ho! Hum! Uff! Uff! I guess I'll have some acorns for my breakfast."

It was a very easy matter for Squinty to get his breakfast. He did not have to wash, or comb his hair, or even dress. Just as he was he got up out of his leaf-bed, and began rooting around in the ground for acorns. He soon found all he wanted, and ate them. Then he felt thirsty, so he looked around until he had found another spring of cool water, where he drank as much as he needed.

"And now to go back home, to the boy who taught me tricks," said Squinty to himself. "I guess he is wondering where I am."

And indeed that boy, Bob, and his sisters Mollie and Sallie, were wondering where Squinty was. They saw the open door of the pen, and the boy recalled that he had forgotten to lock it.

"Oh, Squinty is gone!" he cried, and he felt very badly indeed. But I have no time to tell you more of that boy now. I must relate for you the wonderful adventures of Squinty.

Squinty went this way and that through the woods, but he could not find the path that led to his pen. He tried and tried again, but it was of no use.

"Well," said Squinty, at last, sitting down beside a hollow log, "I guess I am lost. That is all there is to it I am lost in the big woods! Oh dear! I almost wish Don, the dog, or the farmer would come and find me now."

He waited, but no one came. He listened but he heard nothing.

"Well, I might as well eat and go to sleep again," said Squinty, "Maybe something will happen then."

Soon he was asleep again. But he was suddenly awakened. He heard a great crashing in the trees over his head.

"Gracious! I hope that isn't a dog after me!" cried the little pig.

He looked up, Squinty did. He saw coming down from the sky, through the branches of the trees, a big round thing, like more than ten thousand rubber balls, made into one. Below the round thing hung a square basket, with many ropes, and other things, fast to it. And in the basket were two men. They looked over the edge of the basket. One of them pulled on a rope, and the big thing, which was a balloon, though Squinty did not know it, came to the ground with a bang.

"Well, at last we have made a landing," said one of the men.

"Yes," said the other. "And we shall have to throw out some bags of sand to go up again."

Squinty did not know what this meant. But I'll explain to you that a "landing" is when a balloon comes down to the ground. And when the men in it want to go up again, they have to toss out some of the bags of sand, or ballast, they carry to make the balloon so light that the gas in it will take it up again.

The men began tossing out the bags of sand. Squinty saw them, but he was not afraid. Why should he be? for no men or boys had ever been cruel to him.

"Uff! Uff!" grunted Squinty, getting up and going over to one of the bags of sand. "Maybe that is good to eat!" he thought. "If it is I will take a bite. I am hungry."

"Oh, look at that pig!" suddenly called one of the men in the balloon basket.

"Sure enough, it is a pig!" exclaimed the other. "And what a comical little chap he is!" he went on. "See the funny way he looks at you."

At that moment Squinty looked up, as he often did, with one eye partly closed, the other open, and with one ear cocked frontwards, and the other backwards.

"Say, he's a cute one all right," said the first man. "Let's take him along."

"What for?" asked his friend. "We'd only have to toss out as much sand as he weighs so we could go up."

"Oh, let's take him along, anyhow," insisted the other. "Maybe he'll be a mascot for us."

"Well, if he's a mascot, all right. Then we'll take him. We need some good luck on this trip."

Squinty did not know what a mascot was. Perhaps he thought it was something good to eat. But I might say that a mascot is something which some persons think brings them good luck. Often baseball nines, or football elevens, will have a small boy, or a goat, or a dog whom they call their mascot. They take him along whenever they play games, thinking the mascot helps them to win. Of course it really does not, but there is no harm in a mascot, anyhow.

"Yes, we'll take him along in the balloon with us," said the taller of the two men. "See, he doesn't seem to be a bit afraid."

"No, and look! He must be a trick pig! Maybe he got away from some circus!" cried the other man. For, at that moment Squinty stood up on his hind legs, as the boy had taught him, and walked over toward the big balloon basket. What he really wanted was something to eat, but the men did not know that.

"He surely is a cute little pig!" cried the tall man. "I'll lift him in. You toss out another bag of sand, and we'll go up."

The next moment, before he could get out of the man's grasp if he had wanted to, Squinty felt himself lifted off the ground. He was put down in the bottom of the basket, which held many things, and, a second later, Squinty, the comical pig, felt himself flying upward through the air.

Squinty was off on a trip in a balloon.

CHAPTER X

SQUINTY AND THE SQUIRREL

Up, up, and up some more went Squinty, the comical pig. At first the fast motion in the balloon made him a little dizzy, just as it might make you feel queer the first time you went on a merry-go-'round.

"Uff! Uff!" grunted Squinty. He was so surprised at this sudden adventure that, really, he did not know what to say.

"I wonder if he's afraid?" said one of the men.

"He acts so," the other answered. "But he'll get used to it. How high up are you going?"

"Oh, about a mile, I guess."

Squinty cuddled down in the basket of the balloon, between two bags full of something, and shivered.

"My goodness me!" thought poor Squinty. "A mile up in the air! That's awfully high."

He knew about how far a mile was on land, for it was about the distance from the farmhouse, near where his pen used to be, to the village church. He had often heard the farmer man say so.

"And if it was a mile from my pen to the church, and that mile of road was stood straight up in the air," thought Squinty, "it would be a terrible long way to fall. I hope I don't fall."

And it did not seem as if he would--at least not right away. The basket in which he was riding looked good and strong. Squinty had shut his eyes when he heard the men speak about going a mile up in the air, but now, as the balloon seemed to have stopped rising, the little pig opened his eyes again, and peered all about him.

"Look!" exclaimed one of the men with a laugh. "Hasn't that pig the most comical face you ever saw?"

"That's what he has," answered the other. "He makes me want to laugh every time I look at him, with that funny half-shut eye of his."

"Well," thought Squinty, "I'm glad somebody is happy and jolly, and wants to laugh, for I'm sure I don't. I wish I hadn't run away from the nice boy who taught me the tricks."

Then, as Squinty remembered how he had been taught to stand up on his hind legs, he thought he would do that trick now. He was hungry, and he imagined, perhaps, if he did that trick, the men would give him something to eat.

"Look at the little chap!" cried one of the men. "He's showing off all right."

"Yes, he's a smart pig," said the other. "He must be a trick pig, and I guess whoever owns him will be sorry he is lost."

"Hu! I'm sorry myself!" thought Squinty to himself, as he walked around on his hind legs.

"I wonder if these men are ever going to give me anything to eat," he went on. He looked at them from his queer, squinting eye, but the men did not seem to know that the little pig was hungry.

On and on sailed the balloon, being blown by the wind like a sailboat. Squinty dropped down on his four legs, since he found that walking on his hind ones brought him no food. Then, as he made his way about the basket, he saw some more of those queer bags filled with something. There were a great many of them in the balloon, and Squinty thought they must have something good in them.

Squinty squatted down beside one, and, with his strong teeth, he soon had bitten a hole in the cloth. Then he took a big bite, but oh dear!

All at once he found his mouth filled with coarse sand, that gritted on his teeth, and made the cold shivers run down his back.

"Oh, wow!" thought poor Squinty. "That's no good! Sand! I wonder if those men eat sand?"

Of course they didn't. The sand in the bags was "ballast." The balloon men carried it with them, and when they found the balloon coming down, because some of the gas had leaked out of the round ball above the basket, they would let some of the sand run out of the bags to the ground below. This would make the balloon lighter, and it would rise again.

"Squee! Squee! Uff! Uff!" grunted Squinty, as he wiped the sand off his tongue on one of his legs. "I don't like that. I'm hungry."

"Why, what's the matter with the little pig?" asked one of the men, turning around and looking at Squinty.

"He must be hungry," said the other. "See, he has bitten a hole in one of our sand bags. Let's feed him."

"All right. Give him something to eat, but we didn't bring any pig food along with us."

"I'll give him some bread and milk," the other man said. "We won't want much more ourselves, for we are nearly at our last landing place."

"Squee! Squee!" squealed Squinty, when he heard this. He watched the man put some bread and milk in a tin pan, and set it down on the floor of the basket. Then Squinty put his nose in the dish and began to eat.

And Oh! how good it tasted! Of course the milk was sweet, instead of sour, for men do not usually like sour milk. Squinty had a good meal, and then he went to sleep.

What happened while Squinty slept, the little pig did not know. But when he woke up it was all dark, and he knew it must be night, so he went to sleep again. And the next time he awakened the sun was shining, so he felt sure it was morning.

And then, all of a sudden, something happened. One of the men called out:

"There is a good place to land!"

"Yes, we'll go down there," agreed the other. Then he pulled a string. Squinty did not know what it was for, but I'll tell you. It was to open a hole in the balloon so the gas would rush out. Then the balloon would begin to fall.

And that is what happened. Down, down went the balloon. It went very fast, and Squinty felt dizzy. Faster and faster fell the balloon, until, at last it gave such a bump down on the ground that Squinty was bounced right over the side of the basket.

Right out of the basket the comical little pig was bounced, but he came down in a soft bed of leaves, so he was not hurt in the least. He landed on his feet, just like a cat, and gave a loud squeal, he was so surprised.

And then Squinty ran away. Almost anybody would have run, too, I guess, after falling down in a balloon, and being bounced out that way. Squinty had had enough of balloon riding.

"I don't know where I'm going, nor what will happen to me now," thought Squinty, "but I am going to run and hide."

And run he did. He found himself in the woods; just the same kind of woods as where he had first met the two balloon men, only, of course, it was much farther off, for he had traveled a long way through the air.

On and on ran Squinty. All at once, in a tree over his head, he heard a funny chattering noise.

"Chipper, chipper, chipper! Chat! Chat! Whir-r-r-r-!" went the noise.

Squinty looked up in the tree, and there he saw a lovely little girl squirrel, frisking about on the branches. Then Squinty was no longer afraid. Out of the leaves he jumped, giving a squeal and a grunt which meant:

"Oh, how do you do? I am glad to see you. My name is Squinty. What is your name?"

"My name is Slicko," answered the lively little girl squirrel, as she jumped about. "Come on and play!"

Squinty felt very happy then.

CHAPTER XI

SQUINTY AND THE MERRY MONKEY

"Where do you live, Squinty?" asked Slicko, the jumping squirrel, as she skipped from one tree branch to another, and so reached the ground near the comical little pig.

"Oh, I live in a pen," answered Squinty, "but I'm not there now."

"No, I see you are not," spoke Slicko, with a laugh, which showed her sharp, white teeth. "But what are you doing so far away from your pen? Or, perhaps it is close by, though I never saw you in these woods before," she went on, looking around as if she might see the pig pen under one of the trees.

"No, I have never been here before," Squinty answered. "My pen is far from here. My master is a boy who taught me to do tricks, such as jumping rope, but I ran away and had a balloon ride."

"What's a balloon?" asked Slicko, as she combed out her tail with a chestnut burr. Squirrels always use chestnut burrs for combs.

"A balloon is something that goes up in the air," answered Squinty, "and it has bags of sand in it."

"Well, I can go up in the air, when I climb a tree," went on Slicko, with a jolly laugh. "Am I a balloon?"

"No, you are not," said Squinty. "A balloon is very different."

"Well, I know where there is some sand," spoke Slicko. "I could get some of that and put it in leaf-bags. Would that make me a balloon?"

"Oh, no, of course not," Squinty answered. "You could never be a balloon. But if you know where there is some sand perhaps you know where there is some sour milk. I am very hungry."

"I never heard of sour milk," replied the girl squirrel. "But I know where to find some nuts. Do you like hickory nuts?"

"I--I guess so," answered Squinty, thinking, perhaps, they were like acorns. "Please show me where there are some."

61

"Come on!" chattered Slicko. She led the way through the woods, leaping from one tree branch to another over Squinty's head. The little pig ran along on the ground, through the dry leaves. Sometimes he went on four feet and sometimes he stood up straight on his hind feet.

"Can you do that?" he asked the squirrel. "It is a trick the boy taught me."

"Oh, yes, I can sit up on my hind legs, and eat a nut," the squirrel girl said. "But nobody taught me. I could always do it. I don't call that a trick."

"Well, it is a trick for me," said Squinty. "But where are the hickory nuts you spoke of?"

"Right here," answered Slicko, the jumping squirrel, hopping about as lively as a cricket, and she pointed to a pile of nuts in a hollow stump. Squinty tried to chew some, but, as soon as he took them in his mouth he cried out:

"Oh my! How hard the shells are! This is worse than the sand! I can't chew hickory nuts! Have you no other kind?"

"Oh, yes, I know where there are some acorns," answered Slicko, "but I do not care for them as well as for hickory nuts."

"Oh, please show me the acorns," begged Squinty.

"Here they are," spoke Slicko, jumping a little farther, and she pointed to a pile of acorns in another hollow stump.

"Oh, these are fine! Thank you!" grunted Squinty, and he began to eat them. All at once there sounded through the woods a noise like:

"Chat! Chat! Chatter! Whir-r-r-r-r!" "My, what's that?" cried Squinty, turning quickly around.

"That is my mamma calling me," said Slicko, the jumping squirrel. "I shall have to go home to my nest now. Good-by, Squinty. I like you very much, and I hope I shall soon see you again."

"I hope so, too," spoke Squinty, and while he went on eating the acorns, Slicko ran along the tree branches to her nest. And in another book I shall tell you some more stories about "Slicko, the Jumping Squirrel," but in this book I have room to write only about Squinty.

The little comical pig was rather lonesome after Slicko had left him, but he was no longer hungry, thanks to the acorns.

So he walked on and on, and pretty soon he came to a road. And down the road he saw coming the strangest sight.

There were a lot of big wagons, all painted red and green and gold. Many horses drew each wagon, the big wheels of which rattled like thunder, and beside the wagons there were many strange animals walking along--animals which Squinty had never seen before.

"Oh my!" cried Squinty. "This is worse than the balloon! I must run away!"

But, just as he turned to run, he saw a little animal jump out of one of the big wagons, and come toward him. This animal was something like a little boy, only, instead of clothes, he was covered with hairy fur. And the animal had a long tail, which Squinty knew no boy ever had.

Squinty was so surprised at seeing the strange animal that the little pig stood still. The hairy animal, with the long tail, came straight for the bush behind which Squinty was hiding, and crawled through. Then the two stood looking at one another, while the big wagons rumbled past on the road.

"Hello!" Squinty finally exclaimed. "Who are you?"

"Why, I am Mappo, the merry monkey," was the answer, as he curled his long tail around a stick of wood. "But I don't need to ask who you are. You are a pig, I can see that, for we have one in our circus, and the clown rides him around the ring, and it is too funny for anything."

"Ha, so you are a monkey?" asked Squinty. "But what do you mean by a circus?"

"That's a circus," answered Mappo, pointing with one paw through a hole in the bush, at the queer animals, and the red, gold and green wagons. "That is, it will be a circus when they put up the big tent, and all the people come. Didn't you ever see a circus?"

"Never," answered Squinty. "Did you ever ride in a balloon?"

"Never," answered Mappo.

"Well, then we are even," said Squinty. "Now you tell me about a circus, and I'll tell you about the balloon."

"Well," said the monkey, "a circus is a big show in a tent, to make people laugh. There are clowns, and animals to look at. I am one of the animals, but I ran out of my cage when the door flew open."

"Why did you run away?" asked Squinty.

"Oh, I got tired of staying in a cage. And I was afraid the big tiger might bite me. I'll run back again pretty soon, before they miss me. Now you tell me about your balloon ride."

So Squinty told the merry monkey all about running away, and learning tricks, and having a ride in the queer basket.

"I can do tricks, too," said Mappo. "But just now I am hungry. I wonder if any cocoanut trees are in these woods?"

"I don't know what a cocoanut is," answered Squinty, "but I'll give you some of my acorns."

The comical little pig and the merry monkey hid under the bush and ate acorns as they watched the circus procession go past. It was not a regular parade, as the show was going only from one town to-another. Squinty looked at the beautiful wagons, and at the strange animals, some with big humps on their backs. At last he saw some very big creatures, and he cried out:

"Oh, Mappo! What are those animals? They have a tail at each end!"

"Those are elephants," said Mappo, "and they do not have two tails. One is a tail, and the other is their trunk, or long nose, by which they pick up peanuts, and other things to eat, and they can drink water through it, too."

"Oh, elephants, eh!" exclaimed Squinty. "But who is that big, fierce-looking one, with two long teeth sticking out. I would be afraid of him."

"Ha! Ha! You wouldn't need to be," said Mappo, with a merry laugh. "That is Tum-Tum, the jolliest elephant in the whole circus. Why, he is so kind he wouldn't hurt a fly, and he is so happy that every one loves him. He is always playing jokes."

"Well, I'm glad he is so jolly," spoke Squinty, as he watched Tum-Tum and the other elephants march slowly along the road on their big feet, like wash tubs, swinging their long trunks.

Then Mappo the monkey, and Squinty, the comical pig, started off through the woods.

CHAPTER XII

SQUINTY GETS HOME AGAIN

"Squinty, I don't believe we're going to find any cocoanut trees in this woods," said Mappo, the monkey, after he and the little pig had wandered on for some time.

"It doesn't seem so, does it?" spoke Squinty, looking all around, first with his wide-open eye, and then with his queer, droopy one.

The monkey ran along, now on the ground, and now and then swinging himself up in the branches of trees, by his long legs, each one of which had a sort of hand on the end. Sometimes he hung by his tail, for monkeys are made to do that.

"My, I wish I could get up in the trees the way you do," said Squinty. "Do you think I could hang by my tail, Mappo?"

"I don't know," answered the monkey, scratching his head. "Your tail has a nice little curl in it, almost like mine. Did you ever try to hang by your tail?"

"No, I never did."

"Well, you don't know what you can do until you try," said Mappo.

The two animal friends soon came to where some of the acorn nuts had fallen off a tree, and they ate as many as they wanted. Mappo said they were not as good as cocoanuts, but he liked them pretty well, because he was hungry. And Squinty thought acorns were just the best things he had ever tasted, except apples, and potatoes or perhaps sour milk.

By this time it was getting dark, and Squinty said:

"Oh dear, I wonder where we can sleep tonight?"

"Oh, do not let that worry you," said Mappo. "I am used to living in the woods. When I was little, before I was caught and put in the circus, I lived in the woods all the while. See, here is a nice hollow stump, filled with leaves, for you to sleep in, and I will climb a tree, and sleep in that."

"Couldn't you sleep down in the stump with me?" asked Squinty. "It's sort of lonesome, all by yourself in the dark."

"Yes, I'll sleep with you," said Mappo. "Now we'll make up a nice bed."

But, just as they were piling some more leaves in the hollow stump, they heard many voices of men shouting in the woods.

"Here he is! Here is that runaway monkey! I see him! Come and catch him!" cried the men.

"Oh, they're from the circus! They're after me!" cried Mappo. "I must run and hide. Good-by, Squinty. I'll see you again sometime, maybe. You had better run, also, or the circus men may catch you."

Squinty looked through the trees, and saw a number of men coming toward him and the monkey. Then Mappo climbed up in a tall tree, and Squinty ran away as fast as his little short legs would take him.

"Never mind the pig! Get the monkey!" Squinty heard one man cry, and then the comical little pig dodged under a bush, and kept on running.

When Squinty stopped running it was quite dark. He could hardly see, and he had run into several trees, and bumped his nose a number of times. It hurt him very much.

"Well, I guess I'm lost again," thought Squinty. "And I am all alone. Oh, what a lot of things has happened to me since I was in the pen with my mamma and papa and sisters and brothers! I wish I were back with them again."

Squinty felt very sad and lonesome. He wondered if the circus men had caught Mappo. Then he felt that he had better find a place where he could cover himself up with the dry leaves, and go to sleep.

He walked about in the dark until, all of a sudden, he stumbled into a hole that was filled with dried grass.

"I guess I had better stay here," thought Squinty. So he pulled some of the grass over him, and went to sleep.

When he awoke the sun was shining.

"I must get my breakfast," thought Squinty. He hunted about until he had found some acorns, and then, coming to a little brook of water he took a long drink. Something about the brook made Squinty look at it carefully.

"Why--why!" he exclaimed to himself: "It seems to me I have been here before! Yes, I am sure I have. This is the place where I first came to get a drink, when first I ran away. It is near the pen where I used to live! Oh, I wonder if I can find that?"

The heart of Squinty was beating fast as he looked around at the scenes he had seen when he was a very little pig, some weeks before. Yes, it was the same brook. He was sure of it. And there was the garden of potatoes, and the cornfield where he had first lost his way.

Hark! What was that?

Off in the rows of corn he heard a dog barking. Somehow he knew that dog's bark.

"If that could be Don!" thought Squinty, hopefully.

The barking sounded nearer. Squinty turned around, standing on the edge of the little brook, and waited, his heart beating faster and faster.

All at once there came running through the potato field a black and white dog. Squinty knew him at once.

It was Don!

"Bow wow! Bow wow!" barked Don. "Well, if there isn't that comical little pig, Squinty! Where in the world did you come from? You've been running away, I'll be bound! Now I'm going to take you back to the pen!"

"Oh, Don! I am so glad to see you!" squealed Squinty. "I--I did run away, but I never will any more. I am lost. Oh, Don, don't take me by the ear. I'll go with you."

"All right," barked Don, kindly. "Come along. Your pen isn't far off," and he ran along beside the little pig, who, after many adventures had wandered back home. Squinty and Don came to the edge of the potato field.

"Well, I never!" exclaimed the farmer man, who was there hoeing the potatoes. "If there isn't that comical little pig I sold to that boy Bob. I wonder where he came from?"

"Bow wow! Bow wow! I found him," barked Don, but of course the farmer did not understand.

"Well, I'll put you back in the pen again until that boy sends for you," said the farmer, as he lifted Squinty over into the pen where his mamma and papa and brothers and sisters were.

"Why--why, it's Squinty!" cried Mrs. Pig.

"He's come back!" grunted Mr. Pig.

"Oh, I'm so glad!" said Wuff-Wuff.

"And so am I," added Twisty Tail, as she rubbed her nose against Squinty's. "Where have you been, and what happened to you?" she asked her brother.

"Oh, many things," he said. "I have learned some tricks, I have been up in a balloon, I met Slicko the jumping squirrel, Mappo, the merry monkey, and I saw Tum-Tum, the jolly circus elephant. Now I am home again."

"And which did you like best of all?" asked Mrs. Pig, when they had finished asking him questions.

"Getting back home," answered Squinty, as he took a big drink of sour milk.

And that is the story of Squinty, the comical pig. The farmer sent word to the boy that his pet was back in the pen, but the boy said he thought he did not want a pet pig any more, so Squinty, for the time being, stayed with his family.